NANCY SHAW

Raccoon Tune

ILLUSTRATED BY
HOWARD FINE

Henry Holt and Company • New York

Henry Holt and Company, LLC
Publishers since 1866
115 West 18th Street
New York, New York 10011
www.henryholt.com

Library of Congress Cataloging-in-Publication Data
Shaw, Nancy (Nancy E.)
Raccoon tune / by Nancy Shaw; illustrated by Howard Fine.
Summary: A family of raccoons prowls around a neighborhood making a ruckus until they find supper.
[1. Raccoons—Fiction. 2. Stories in rhyme.] I. Fine, Howard, ill. II. Title.
PZ8.3.S5334 Rac 2003   [E]—dc21   2002005945

ISBN 0-8050-6544-X
First Edition—2003
Printed in the United States of America on acid-free paper. ∞

10 9 8 7 6 5 4 3 2 1

The artist used oil paint on gessoed paper to create the illustrations for this book.

To Colette Weber Shaw and the Moot family
— N. S.

In memory of Harry Devlin —
I hope that he would have approved
— H. F.

Moonlight,
June night,
Just-right-for-raccoon night.

Not too dark,
Not too bright,
As we look for treats.

Out we creep
While people sleep.
Soon we hope to find a heap
Of cheese and bread crumbs,
Piled deep
On codfish bones and beets.

Deep in bins we always forage,
Clanking tins we find in storage—
Apple skins and maple porridge,
Broccoli and sweets.

Ash cans.

Trash cans.

How we love to crash cans,

Mash and smash and bash cans.

We'll get that lid to pop!

We have to throw it at the fence.
People should have common sense.
There wouldn't be so many dents
If they'd leave off the top.

This lid is on a little tight.

We'll have to put up quite a fight.

We pull

    and pull

        with all our might.

But nothing gives until . . .

We grab the can and try to spin it.
The top comes off.
Look what's in it!

Oh, no!

It's rolling down the hill!

We thought we saw some cake with cream,

Or was that just a hungry dream?

It's rolling fast and gathering steam.

We run!

We dash!

A clunk!

A splash!

Our tasty trash

Has fallen in the stream.

Dive right in and grab it!

Quick!

Teamwork ought to do the trick.

Hook a handle!

Poke a stick!

At last we pull it out.

Oh, my whiskers!
How delish!
The can is full of flopping fish.
A super-duper supper dish!
We'll have a feast of trout.

Moonlight,
June night,
Just-right-for-raccoon night.
Not too dark,
Not too bright . . .

When we are dining out.